Till The Last Moment

ZAKIR JAWED BHATTI

Copyright © 2025 by Zakir Jawed Bhatti

All rights reserved. No part of this publication may be reproduced, stored or transmitted in any form or by any means, photocopying, scanning, electronic, mechanical, recording, or otherwise without written permission from the publisher.

ISBN: 978-1-0691981-2-9

To my wife

Table of Contents

Chapter 1.	Single and Not Ready to Mingle	5
Chapter 2.	All My Accidents Lead to You	13
Chapter 3.	Pie, Cholesterol, and You	20
Chapter 4.	You, Me, and the Calgary Rain	26
Chapter 5.	Second Chances and First Loves	36
Chapter 6.	This Is What Love Looks Like	44
Chapter 7.	The Proposal That Almost Was	52
Chapter 8.	When the Rain Fell Hardest	65
Chapter 9.	By Your Side, No Matter What	77
Chapter 10.	Walking Down the Aisle of Time	85

Chapter 1

Single and Not Ready to Mingle

It was a quiet afternoon on the University of Calgary campus. The garden near MacKimmie Tower was peaceful, with only the soft rustling of leaves and the occasional chirp of birds breaking the silence.

Anna sat alone on a bench, shoulders trembling as she sobbed into her sleeves. At just sixteen and in her first year of early college entry, heartbreak felt like the end of the world. Irena—two years older, street-smart, and always calm—sat beside her with a comforting arm around her.

"No, Anna," Irena said gently, brushing a strand of hair from Anna's face. "Everything will be okay."

Footsteps crunched along the gravel path. Monica and Sophia, both nineteen, approached, bundled in light fall jackets against the Calgary chill.

"What's wrong with our baby?" Monica asked playfully, her tone softening as she knelt in front of Anna.

Earlier that day, outside the Taylor Family Digital Library, Anna had been lingering nervously when a handsome boy she'd been seeing walked up. The sun had just peeked through the clouds after a light morning snowfall, and the air still smelled like fresh frost.

"Have you eaten already?" he asked, hands shoved into the pockets of his hoodie.

"No," Anna replied. "Let's eat."

They entered the nearby campus café—warm, buzzing with conversation, and rich with the scent of brewed coffee and toasted sandwiches. They found a quiet table near the window. For a moment, Anna felt safe. Then he looked up, eyes suddenly serious.

"Anna, let's break up."

Her smile faded. She stared at him, lips parting slightly, tears stinging the corners of her eyes.

"Why? I can do better… can't I?"

He sighed. "I still like you. You make me happy. I'm always comfortable when you're around."

"Then why?" she whispered.

"You're always busy with your studies. Nothing exciting is happening. This is college—it's our chance to have fun. Time is flying, babe."

"But we're students," Anna replied. "Shouldn't studying be our priority?"

He shrugged. "So go ahead and study… I just don't want to waste time."

Then he stood and walked out, leaving Anna sitting in silence, heart cracked open under the café's warm lights.

Now, back in the garden's fading sunlight, Anna wiped her tears. Monica, always the joker in tense moments, slid a hand playfully across Anna's back and smirked.

"The rat dumped you. So what? Now you've got time to find someone actually worth it."

Anna looked at her—half in disbelief, half trying not to smile.

That evening, the four walked along the Bow River near Prince's Island Park. The sun dipped low, casting orange streaks across the water, and the breeze smelled like pine and wet leaves. A crisp Calgary evening hinted that winter was near.

"There are two types of boys," Monica said, leaning closer to Anna. "The ones who treat you like a princess… and the ones you're better off without. You learn something from both."

Anna stayed quiet, but the sadness in her eyes had softened.

Monica grinned. "Okay, enough of this, time to throw Anna in the water!"

Anna shrieked and tried to run, but Monica caught her arm, laughing. The others followed, shoes crunching over pebbles as they dragged her to the riverbank.

"Put your hands in," Monica said.

Anna dipped her hands into the cold river and gasped.

"Fish," she laughed. "I feel fish."

"There are tons of them," Monica said. "So don't cry over the one you didn't catch."

She looked out over the glowing water, voice thoughtful.

"As for me, the idea of being with one person forever doesn't make sense. But I still respect marriage—for those who choose it."

The river flowed quietly beside them. For the first time that day, Anna felt like maybe things would be okay.

That was the last time the four stood by the Bow River together... until now.

***

Twenty-one years later, Anna, Sophia, and Monica sat at a round table in a cozy downtown Calgary café bar. Each held a glass of wine. A rich chocolate cake topped with four flickering candles sat in the center. Golden pendant lights cast a warm glow. Soft jazz played in the background.

"To Monica," Anna said, raising her glass. "Go on, blow out the candles."

"Wait," Monica smiled. "Irena will be here soon."

Just then, Irena burst through the door, breathless but radiant.

"I had to leave my kids with my idiot husband just to be here," she said. "That man drives them nuts. And me too."

Later, they clapped and sang as Monica leaned forward and blew out the candles. Cheers erupted. Anna returned with a tray of drinks, eyes sparkling as she set the glasses down.

Irena nudged Monica. "Don't you think it's time you found yourself a man to settle down with?"

Anna scowled. "And end up with someone like your husband, who specializes in driving everyone nuts?"

They all laughed.

"He's not as bad as I make him sound," Irena said. "Back in 1950, women married at twenty. Last year? Twenty-seven. Thanks to women like you, Monica, it'll be forty next year."

Monica rolled her eyes. "Why do you all offer marriage advice like you're certified therapists?"

Sophia grinned. "I thought you were holding out for Mr. Perfect."

"At first, yeah," Monica said. "Then my twenties turned into my thirties, and I got less open to the whole thing. Now that I'm in my forties... even if I met the love of my life, I doubt I'd want to marry."

Irena frowned. "So you don't think there's happiness in marriage?"

"I think there is—for some. And I wish them joy. But marriage isn't just about love. It's sharing time, money, your most personal self. I'm too possessive for that."

"Don't you ever think," Irena asked, swirling her wine, "that being single too long might mean living—and dying—alone?"

"I know it gets lonely," Monica admitted. "But the problems I face are mine alone. And that makes me content."

Irena smirked. "I was just kidding—why go all philosopher on me? Anyway, I have to go. Time to put the kids to sleep and cradle my husband's... well, you know." She winked.

Anna and Sophia burst out laughing. "You've made Monica jealous," Anna said. "She's turning green."

"Envious?" Monica scoffed, "hardly. Let's hit the bar. Bye, Irena!"

After goodbyes, the three moved to the bar. A handsome man sat alone on a stool, sipping a smoothie. His sharp jawline, salt-and-pepper stubble, and easy air made him stand out.

Sophia nudged Anna. "Let's dare Monica to talk to him. Maybe she'll marry him."

"Oh, shut up," Monica muttered.

Anna grinned. "Let's see if you can land a kiss on his cheek in five minutes."

"I'm in," Monica said, "but you two are paying for movies and dinner next time."

"Done," they said in unison.

Monica walked to the bar, pretending not to notice the man. Instead, she approached the bartender.

"Hi, what can I get you?" bartender asked.

Monica nodded at the man. "I'll try whatever he's drinking."

"One smoothie coming up," bartender said.

She sipped slowly. Minutes passed. Then she stood and walked toward the man, who had also just stood.

She stumbled. Her hand clutched his back. In a moment of chaos, she collapsed.

The man turned just in time to catch her and gently lowered her to the ground.

"Are you okay?" he asked, supporting her.

Anna and Sophia rushed over.

"What's wrong, Monica?" they cried.

Monica's lips trembled. "Pea… pea… peanuts…"

"Are you allergic?" the man asked urgently.

Monica nodded.

He called for an ambulance. "Don't worry. I'm a doctor. She's in safe hands."

In the dim hospital room, Monica lay under a blanket, an IV in her arm. A nurse entered with the man.

"Well, Nurse Joanita, what did the medics say?" he asked.

"They gave her cortisone, Doctor Chandler. Here are her files."

As Chandler scanned the papers, one name jumped out: Monica Allen. A name he hadn't seen in twenty years. He remembered it clearly.

***

They were nineteen, standing on a terrace under the Calgary stars. Monica kissed him tenderly.

"Monica!" a voice yelled.

"I'm coming, Grandma!" she called.

Later, she found him still staring up.

"What are you looking at?" Monica asked, stepping up beside him.

"That bright one," Chandler said, pointing toward the sky. "Maybe it is a shooting star?"

"No," she said, "too steady. It is probably a satellite."

"That's probably why none of my wishes come true," he muttered. "I've been wishing on satellites."

She kissed his back and hugged him.

That night, she'd snuck him out quietly. Her parents had been arguing—loud and bitter.

"That happens almost every day," she whispered, not meeting his eyes. "They can't stand each other."

Now, twenty-one years later, Chandler held that same girl—now a woman—in his arms again, stunned by the weight of memory.

Chapter 2

All My Accidents Lead to You

Back in the present, Chandler let out a sigh. Monica stirred beneath the blanket.

He watched her with quiet awe. So much had changed over the past twenty years.

"Did you say something, Doctor?" she murmured.

"Yes, Monica. I'm your doctor—Chandler Wood. The same guy you tried to flirt with."

"Chandler? I didn't recognize you! And last night… that was just a dare gone wrong"

Chandler chuckled. "Get some rest."

He stepped into the waiting area, where Anna and Sophia were seated.

"Is she okay?" Anna asked.

"She'll be fine," Chandler replied. "Turns out the drink she ordered had traces of peanuts—and she's allergic. But I don't get it—why order a nutty cocktail if you're allergic?"

Sophia shrugged. "That's what happens when someone goes nuts over a different kind of nut."

She made a playful gesture, and Anna burst out laughing.

Chandler shook his head, a smile tugging at his lips.

When they returned to Monica's room, she was attempting to pull out the IV.

"Seriously," Chandler said. "You and nuts clearly don't get along, and now you're acting like a nutcase. Can't handle a needle prick?"

Monica pointed to the drip. "The medicine's finished."

Chandler checked. "Ok Fair enough. But let us handle it—that's why we're here. Now, sit still."

He wrapped the blood pressure cuff around her arm.

"Deep breath... and let it out."

After a moment, he removed the cuff.

"You'll need rest for a few days. We've run some precautionary tests, but don't worry."

He gave her one last glance before stepping out with Anna and Sophia.

***

Chandler entered his apartment just as the city lights flickered on beyond his floor-to-ceiling windows. The space was clean, minimalist—everything in its place.

He loosened his tie, set his keys on the glass countertop, and headed to the bathroom. Steam soon filled the room as hot water cascaded over his body. The muscles along his back flexed with each breath—lean and defined, the result of years of disciplined workouts. His movements were methodical, almost meditative, as though the routine grounded him.

After drying off, he changed into a plain black T-shirt and joggers then padded barefoot into the kitchen. He opened the fridge, pulled out seasoned salmon and vegetables, and began to cook. Within minutes, the air filled with the rich aroma of garlic and rosemary.

Once plated, he poured a glass of red wine, letting it breathe as he set the needle on his old phonograph. A smooth jazz record hummed to life, the soft crackle of vinyl warming the silence.

He walked over to the bookshelf lining the wall. His fingers drifted across familiar titles before settling on a dog-eared novel. He returned to the couch, wine resting nearby, and opened the book.

His eyes scanned the pages, but his mind wandered.

I feel lonely tonight... but why? Didn't I promise myself I'd live a great life—healthy, happy—even if it meant doing it alone?

The thought lingered, heavier than expected. Maybe it was seeing Monica again. Maybe it was how familiar her name still sounded after all these years.

He took a sip of wine, but the warmth didn't reach the weight in his chest.

The next morning, Chandler, Michael, and a few women were in the hospital elevator. It beeped repeatedly—overloaded.

The women glanced at the men, waiting for someone to step out. When another woman arrived, Michael exited and nudged Chandler to follow. Chandler stayed.

"Wasn't that your friend?" one woman asked Michael.

Michael smirked. "Yes. We usually avoid the same elevator."

Chandler arrived at Monica's hospital room—only to find the bed empty. A nurse walked in, holding her chart.

"Where's the patient?" Chandler asked.

"She left," the nurse replied.

"I advised her to stay a few more days," Chandler muttered, scanning the report.

Michael entered, shaking his head. "That's disrespectful, ignoring her doctor's advice... typical B."

Chandler shot him a look. "You're too harsh on Bs."

"B's are bad," Michael declared. "Bitch, Bastard, Bimbo, Battle, Bankruptcy, Bum, Beggar—any good words start with B?"

The nurse winked. "Boobs and butts for starters."

They all laughed, but Chandler's tone turned serious.

"Let's not judge people by their blood types."

***

Later, at the gym, Anna performed her routine, drawing the attention of nearly every man around. One even dropped his weights trying to eavesdrop.

In another section, Susie filmed Sophia.

"Darling, I knew you'd have trouble sleeping on your business trip without me," Sophia cooed into the camera. "But don't worry—I'll show you a couple of bedtime exercises to help you sleep like a baby."

She blew a kiss then demonstrated a stretch. "Lie on your back. Inhale... exhale. Do this three times."

She pulled one leg toward her chest and twisted gently.

"Ouch... nope, that hurts," she said, standing up.

She smiled awkwardly. "Okay, remember: keep your back straight, legs relaxed. Let your body roll forward. Reach for your toes."

As she bent forward, she toppled over, sending nearby gym-goers into fits of laughter.

"Ouch, ouch... That's a no-go. You'll have to delete this one," she said, holding out a hand for Susie.

In another room, Monica, Irena, and others were on treadmills.

"I'm amazed you find time to work out with all your kids," Monica said.

Irena smiled. "Being a housewife is the hardest job in the world. Being a mother is even harder. If you stop caring for yourself, it affects how you care for your family. Looking after your body makes you a better wife and mother."

Monica nodded, but her attention drifted to two curvy women increasing their treadmill speed. Trying to keep up, Monica cranked hers too high, lost balance, and fell hard—striking her forehead.

She was rushed to the hospital.

Chandler entered Monica's room after the ambulance brought her in.

She woke groggy and confused, spotting Chandler beside her.

"What happened? Where am I?"

"You're safe," Chandler said gently.

She tried to sit up, but he motioned for her to stay down. Michael entered moments later.

"I advise you to stay the night at the hospital. You left—and now you're back again?" Chandler asked, eyeing her with concern.

"I don't like hospitals," Monica muttered.

"No one likes hospitals," he said gently. "Anyway, tell me—what happened?"

Irena quickly explained. Chandler chuckled, but Monica glared at him.

"Why didn't you listen to your doctor?" he asked, checking her pulse.

Hours later, near the end of his shift, Chandler returned to check on her. Monica was sweating heavily. He wiped her forehead with a handkerchief. As his hand touched her skin, she suddenly gripped his tightly. He paused.

A memory flashed. Monica was in the backseat of a car. Her mother was driving. A bus ahead slammed its brakes. Their car crashed into a truck.

Monica jolted awake.

"It's you," she whispered, recognizing Chandler sitting by her bed.

He looked at her with concern. "You don't seem fine."

She shook her head. "Yes… I'm fine."

"Nightmare?"

"No," she lied.

"You can tell me. We all have them—bad memories we wish we could forget. I have one too," he said softly.

Monica hesitated. "It's my mom. She died in a car accident. I was in the car. I couldn't sleep for years. Then it stopped. But now… it's back. I don't know why."

Chandler nodded. "Maybe stress. Are you dealing with anything right now?"

"No," Monica whispered. "I'm happy."

And just like that, she drifted back to sleep, Chandler still seated beside her, holding her hand.

Chapter 3

Pie, Cholesterol, and You

Chandler woke up in the hospital room just as the morning shift staff began arriving. He heard soft sound and turning to his side saw Monica's face. A small smile tugged at his lips as he gazed at her. His eyes drifted to their hands—his was still holding hers. He quickly stood, startled by the realization, just as the nurse walked in.

"Nurse," Chandler greeted with a brief smile.

"Good morning, Doc," she replied cheerfully.

"Morning," he muttered, trying to shake off the awkwardness. He quickly left the room and headed to the washroom.

Chandler splashed cold water on his face, staring at his reflection in the mirror.

Why on earth did I sleep there last night, holding her hand?

It was unprofessional...

No. I did the right thing. She was struggling. I promised her friends I'd look after her.

He sighed, still tangled in thought. As he dried his hands, Michael appeared, leaning casually against the sink.

"How was your night shift?" Michael asked.

"Same as usual," Chandler mumbled, still distracted.

Without another word, Chandler exited, pushing thoughts of Monica from his mind.

Monica stepped into the hospital hall later that morning, her eyes scanning the busy corridor.

People sat in the waiting area—some chatting, some scrolling through their phones. Her gaze landed on a woman with a toddler in her lap. The child stared at Monica with wide eyes.

Monica made a silly face, crossing her eyes. The child giggled. But as she twisted her nose dramatically, the child suddenly burst into tears.

The mother turned, concerned. "What's wrong?"

Monica gave an apologetic smile and quietly walked back to her room.

She was sitting on her bed when Chandler entered, a stack of reports in hand. His expression was professional as he approached.

"Any pain?" he asked, glancing at her chart.

"No. Is that everything?" Monica asked her tone curious.

"Mostly," Chandler replied, flipping through the papers. "Diagnosis and treatment worked out well."

Monica stood up, stretching. "So I'm free to go?"

"Not yet. Sit down a moment. Let's go over a few things."

She sat back down—perhaps a little too eagerly.

"Your pathology report came back normal, but..." Chandler paused, tapping a line on the paper. "Your cholesterol's at 296. LDL is 188, HDL is 320. That's dangerously high."

"What?" Monica frowned.

"Cholesterol," he clarified. "And your blood pressure's elevated. Factoring in your stress and nightmares, this could lead to serious issues down the line."

"You really like to make things sound worse than they are," Monica said, half-teasing.

Chandler smiled slightly. "Luckily, your weight is normal, but that doesn't guarantee anything. You need to improve your diet and lifestyle."

"Let me guess—cut meat, no smoking, no wine, eat grass and pretend it tastes good?" she said dryly.

"You know the drill."

Monica sighed. "Yeah, but I can't. When I feel like eating, I eat. Why not live until the end? Maybe an early grave isn't so bad."

Chandler studied her, his voice soft. "Were you always like this? Why don't you think about the people who care about you?"

Monica's face faltered the sarcasm slipping. "Don't worry. No one would miss me."

Chandler's voice dropped. "What about your friends?"

She paused, then turned and walked out without answering. The room felt colder in her absence.

That night, Chandler passed by the counter, lost in thought. Michael, still lounging there, raised a curious brow.

"What's going on?"

"Why can't I stop thinking about her?" Chandler murmured, mostly to himself.

"Who?" Michael asked with a grin. "She at least looks good?"

Chandler nodded, distracted. "Yes. But it's her eyes..."

Michael tilted his head. "Her eyes?"

Chandler glanced at him. "Remember what my mom used to say? People with kind eyes have pure hearts."

Michael laughed. "You can't judge someone just by their eyes, man."

Chandler playfully hit Michael on the back. "True, but you judge people by their blood types," he said with a grin.

Two nights later, under a nearly full moon, Monica walked along the sidewalk, drawn by a small crowd on the corner.

She approached a woman standing nearby. "Why is everyone gathered here?"

"They say there'll be shooting stars soon," the woman replied. "People are waiting to make a wish."

Chandler happened to pass by, noticing the crowd. He walked up to a different woman and said, "Those aren't stars. They're satellites. Trust me."

He walked on without seeing Monica, who stood quietly, watching the night sky. A star streaked across the heavens. She clasped her hands together, eyes closed in silent hope.

Later that evening, Monica and Chandler ran into each other at the grocery store, both eyeing the last piece of American pie.

Their hands reached for it at the same time.

"It's you again," Monica said with a smirk.

"Yes. It's me," Chandler replied.

"I took it first."

"No way, I had it first," he said, grinning. "Why not just ask nicely?"

"Why would I do that?" she laughed, trying to wrestle it from him.

They playfully fought over the pie.

"Two adults fighting over dessert, this is embarrassing," Monica said between laughs.

"Then let it go," Chandler said. "Sugar's bad for you, remember? Eat your vegetables."

Still laughing, Monica walked off. Chandler paid quickly and rushed after her.

Outside, he held out the pie, breathless. "Here. Take it."

"No," she replied, waving him off.

"What's your problem? I'm giving it to you."

"Then keep it," she said, smiling slightly. "But thanks."

After a moment, she hesitated and finally accepted the pie.

As Monica walked home, Chandler followed from a short distance. Eventually, she turned around.

"Why are you following me?"

"Don't flatter yourself. I live here," Chandler said with a smirk.

"I think the last time I saw you around here was twenty years ago."

"I just moved back," he explained, falling into step beside her.

They walked in silence, the air between them thick with things unsaid.

At home, Monica went straight to the kitchen. The lights were already on. She sat at the table, eating the pie slowly, savoring each bite.

Later, she grabbed some healthy snacks, turned on romantic music, and curled into bed. As she finished eating, she pulled the blanket over her face.

I'm safe now. I feel peaceful, she thought, drifting into sleep with the lights still glowing.

Chapter 4
You, Me, and the Calgary Rain

Chandler sat quietly on the Open Loop bus, staring out the window. The sprawling Calgary skyline stretched before him, a breathtaking combination of snow-capped peaks and modern cityscapes. His mind wandered, but the serenity was short-lived. Monica stepped onto the bus, and their eyes met instantly.

Chandler quickly looked away. Monica scanned the bus for an empty seat but found none, except the one next to him. After a brief hesitation, she walked over and sat beside him.

"I'm sitting here," she said, almost in a whisper.

"You've already sat down," Chandler replied.

They both fell silent, the awkwardness hanging between them. For a moment, they each tried to pretend the other wasn't there. But then Chandler broke the silence.

"How's your health now?" he asked, his voice low.

"Good, thanks to you," Monica replied with a soft smile. "What a coincidence."

Chandler looked at her, then away. "Have you been on this tour before?"

Monica shook her head. "This is my first time."

Chandler chuckled. "Are you joking? I used to live here twenty years ago. I just recently returned and have already taken a few tours."

Monica smiled. "No, I'm not joking. I always go out with friends, but I never took a bus tour before."

As the bus moved through the city, Chandler and Monica caught glimpses of Calgary's majestic skyline. From the towering glass buildings to the historic streets of downtown, the city was alive with energy.

They both watched in silence, mesmerized by the view of Calgary's beauty. The calm of the moment was soothing. They disembarked at High Line Park, a hidden gem tucked in the middle of Calgary.

Surrounded by greenery and the hum of the city, Monica and Chandler wandered through the park, taking turns snapping photos of each other. They laughed, their shared smiles making the day feel lighter.

Later, they found themselves wandering through the Calgary Farmers' Market. The air was thick with the scent of fresh pastries and street food, the lively chatter of vendors and customers filling the space.

Monica and Chandler walked side by side, sampling treats and enjoying each other's company.

"Calgary certainly is a magnificent place," Monica remarked, glancing around.

Chandler nodded his gaze distant for a moment. "It really is."

As Chandler and Monica made their way back, the sky darkened, and a sudden rainstorm caught them off guard. Monica paused for a moment.

"I'm hungry," she said, glancing at Chandler.

"We just ate so much food," he replied with a laugh, but suddenly, the rain began to pour, cutting their conversation short.

Without warning, Chandler broke into a run, trying to escape the downpour.

"Speed up! That way, you'll dodge the rain!" he called back.

Monica smiled her eyes bright with mischief. "Oh, it's raining. I like rain. Let's walk. I'm tired, I don't want to run."

Despite her words, the rain grew heavier, and Chandler sped up, urging her to keep pace.

"Are you dumb?" he said, shaking his head. "If you get to your destination quickly, you won't be so wet."

Monica couldn't help but laugh as she ran alongside him. Soon, they found shelter under the awning of a nearby house, both of them slightly soaked but relieved. Chandler watched as Monica wiped the rain from her face, her hair damp but still beautiful. For a moment, he was lost in her.

"Gosh, it's pouring," Monica said, laughing softly.

Chandler stepped closer, his gaze fixed on her. His voice was soft, almost hesitant. "Do you want to go out with me?"

Monica blinked in surprise. "Are you crazy?"

Chandler smiled, though there was a nervous edge to his expression. "I'm not crazy... Why does asking you out make me crazy?"

Monica paused, her expression thoughtful. "Yes. What do you know about me? A lot has changed since you left."

Chandler's eyes softened. "What do I need to know?"

Monica stared at the floor for a moment, her voice low and deliberate. "Back then, I really wanted to be a doctor. Like you, Chandler," she said.

She gave a small, almost embarrassed laugh.

"I don't even know why exactly — maybe it was the idea of helping people, of fixing something broken. But I guess I wasn't smart enough."

Her fingers curled slightly in her lap as she continued.

"I took the entrance exams three times. And every time, I thought, this is it. This time I've got it. But I didn't. I never made it."

She looked up, meeting his eyes for a fleeting second before looking away again.

"Exams are hard, aren't they? You study and study until your head feels like it's going to burst, and still — it's not enough."

There was a pause, the kind that stretched not from awkwardness, but from memory.

"By the fourth year, I just... I let go. Figured it wasn't meant to be. So I enrolled in beauty school." Her voice softened. "I thought, maybe if I can't heal people, I can at least help them feel good about themselves."

She smiled faintly at the thought, her expression touched by nostalgia.

"I remember standing in that little salon, learning how to hold scissors properly, how to find the right angle, how to make someone look in the mirror and smile. It felt like something. Like maybe I could be good at it."

Her smile faded. "But now... I'm not so sure."

She hesitated then added, almost in a whisper, "How do I even put this? I don't have the head or the heart for curing people. And maybe I thought I had a sense for beauty — for making others feel seen. But even that feels like a lie some days."

Her gaze dropped to the floor again.

"I wanted to be more," she said. "I really did."

She didn't cry. She didn't ask for comfort. She just stood there.

Chandler moved closer, his hand reaching for hers. His lips brushed against hers, a soft, tentative kiss. For a brief moment, the world around them disappeared.

Monica kissed him back, and this time, it was more than just a fleeting gesture. It was real.

Soon after their passionate kiss, they pulled apart, their hands touching lightly, as if to remind themselves that this moment was theirs alone.

After the rain stopped, Monica and Chandler walk down the quiet street, the moonlight casting a soft glow over them. A moment of silence passes, but it is not uncomfortable. They share a glance, their eyes speaking volumes in the stillness.

***

Next day, Monica cuts the hair of a graceful client, the soft snip of the scissors filling the air. Once she's done, she moves to the corner of the salon, picking up her phone. She dials Chandler's number, the screen lighting up as she waits for him to pick up.

Chandler, still in his scrubs, finishes checking on a patient and bids them farewell. He picks up his phone, glancing at the caller ID before answering.

"Hello?"

"Chandler," Monica's voice is calm but firm on the other end. "We need to talk."

"I'm listening," Chandler replies, concern edging his tone.

"No face-to-face," Monica insists, her words holding a weight that makes Chandler frown.

Chandler and Monica sit at a table by the window in a restaurant. "About last night…" Monica begins, but Chandler interrupts, his eyes sincere.

"Let me speak first," he says, leaning forward slightly. "I like you. What happened last night wasn't a mistake. It wasn't a joke. I meant it. I like you a lot. I think about you constantly—wondering if you've eaten, if you're okay, what you're doing… If you tell me it was a mistake, I'll understand, but please, give me a chance. I'm serious."

Monica listens, her heart racing. The words feel like an answer to something she's been waiting for.

"I feel that way too," she admits quietly. "It wasn't a mistake. I like you, too."

Chandler's face lights up with a smile, and in his excitement, he knocks over a glass of juice, spilling it on her lap.

"Sorry! Sorry," he stammers, his face turning red.

Without missing a beat, he removes his jacket and drapes it over her lap. Monica laughs softly, her heart swelling with affection.

That night, Monica lies on her couch in her apartment, staring at Chandler's jacket draped over the armrest. Her thoughts drift to him, her mind spinning with the emotions he's stirred in her. She bites her lip, a self-conscious smile tugging at her lips.

"Oh, Monica," she whispers to herself, "have you gone crazy?"

The phone rings, interrupting her reverie. It's Chandler.

Chandler stands in his kitchen, chopping vegetables.

"Hi."

"You were thinking about me," Chandler asked.

"No," she'd said, even though they both knew it wasn't true.

"Where do you want to go tomorrow?" He asked.

"Any place you want," she replied without hesitation.

"You decide."

"You already know I'm not good at places. So you decide," Monica answered.

There was a pause, and then his voice again.

"Okay. See you tomorrow. Good night. Sweet dreams."

"You too," She whispered it back, a little softer.

***

After her work finished Monica steps out of the salon to find Chandler waiting outside, a bicycle leaning against the wall. She stops short, surprised to see him in such a casual setting. He flashes a grin.

"Are you ready for a ride?"

Monica hesitates for a moment then grins back. "Sure, why not?"

She climbs onto the back of the bike, wrapping her arms around his waist. They ride off, laughter and lightness in the air.

They arrive at a park, Chandler parking the bicycle and setting down a picnic mat.

The two of them sat together in the garden under a sky streaked with soft golden hues. Flowers swayed in the breeze, and the air smelled of lavender and earth.

It was the kind of moment Monica wished she could bottle and keep forever.

Chandler pulls out a lunch box, revealing a simple but lovingly prepared meal.

"Wow," Monica says, delighted. "I love picnics."

They eat together, surrounded by the beauty of the garden. Chandler watches Monica with a fond smile.

"How's the food?"

"Amazing," Monica exclaims, her eyes wide with appreciation.

Chandler's face softens as he takes her hand. "I cooked it just for you," he says quietly.

"I wanted it to be delicious, but also healthy. Please, always be healthy."

"Is it fun to cook?" she asked, her voice light, curious.

Chandler looked thoughtful for a moment. "I think for me, it's comforting."

"Comforting?" she echoed.

"I see food as a kind of preventive medicine," he said. "Of course, it can't replace real medication, but eating well... it helps. It prevents. It heals—at least in small ways."

Chandler paused, his expression shifting

"When we moved," he began voice quieter now, "my parents divorced. And few years later, my mom got sick. I never knew what would happen to her. The doctor told her she needed rest, so she stopped cooking. We couldn't afford takeout. That's when I started... just doing what I could in the kitchen."

His gaze dropped to his plate, but his thoughts were far away. "That's how I learned—how to make food that was both healthy and tasted good. And maybe that's also why I became a doctor. Seeing people healthy, knowing I had some part in that... it makes me feel grateful. It makes me happy."

Chandler looked up, eyes meeting hers, his voice steady but filled with something deep and personal.

"So don't get sick," he added, almost as a plea.

Before Monica could respond, a soft rumble rolled across the sky, and within moments, raindrops began to fall.

Chandler frowned, standing quickly. He moved to gather their food, stuffing it into a bag and trying to shield it from the rain. But Monica didn't move. She tilted her face up to the sky, laughing quietly as the water soaked her hair, her dress, her skin.

He looked over at her — so carefree, so alive — and something inside him cracked open.

Abandoning the bag, Chandler crossed the distance between them, grabbed her by the waist, and kissed her. Rain streamed down around them, but neither of them cared. The world disappeared in that one, soaked, perfect moment.

As the rain poured, so did the words in his head: *I was empty, alone, lost. Then you came. Like the first rain after drought—you made everything bloom.*

Chapter 5
Second Chances and First Loves

Next day, at the Chinook mall, Monica stands in front of a mirror, trying on various dresses. Irena and Anna are there, offering advice, while Sophia watches with a thoughtful expression. Monica looks radiant, her joy evident in every movement.

"I'm so happy for you… How does it feel to be in love?" Irena says, smiling at Monica as she twirls in the dress.

Monica looks at her reflection, her expression softening. "What love?" she teases, but her smile betrays the truth.

Anna pulls out a red dress, and Monica slips into it. When she emerges, Sophia gasps, her eyes lighting up. "That's it. This one is perfect."

Monica stepped inside, her heart pounding with anticipation. When she reappeared, she was wearing the dress, and Sophia couldn't help but smile.

"Wow, you look amazing," Sophia said.

Monica glanced at herself in the mirror, and her reflection seemed to confirm Sophia's words. "You really think so?"

Sophia nodded. "Now come here."

She walked over to Monica and began to apply makeup, her hands steady and focused. Irena, who had been watching, stepped forward, her voice quiet but thoughtful.

"You know, a woman's heart is often protected by a wall—layers of steel stacked over time. We don't always know what's behind it, or how to break through. But the funny thing about that guarded heart is... it can change in the blink of an eye," Irena said.

Irena's eyes locked with Monica's. "And I can see that change in you."

***

The next morning, Monica stepped out of her apartment building, taking a moment to watch Chandler, who was waiting by his convertible. His presence made her heart skip a beat, a tender smile forming on her lips.

The other women, watching the scene unfold, raised their eyebrows. Chandler, always the gentleman, was holding her bag, and Monica felt a warm surge of affection.

Monica climbed into the car, and as they drove through Calgary's streets, the city's familiar skyline fading in the rearview mirror, she couldn't help but sing along to song playing on the radio.

The breeze tousled her hair, and she smiled, stealing glances at Chandler.

"He's killing me with that smile," she muttered to herself, but her words were lost in the wind.

As they drove further out of the city, the landscape became more rugged, stretching into the wilderness beyond Calgary. Their destination was a Lake Louise, one that Monica had visited before, and she was eager to show Chandler its hidden beauty.

The boat ride was peaceful, the calm water mirroring the clear blue sky. When a wave from a passing boat rocked them gently, Monica couldn't help but lean into Chandler. Their faces were close, and they exchanged shy smiles.

Later, they reached a quiet lake view restaurant. Over lunch, Monica watched as Chandler inhaled the scent of his soup before taking a sip, as if savoring every moment. She mimicked the gesture, intrigued by how it made the food taste better.

"I admit it," Monica said with a grin, "that really does work."

Afterward, they wandered through rock crevices, a local legend promising that wishes made while passing through all six crevices would come true. Hand in hand, they silently made their wishes, the connection between them deepening with each step.

As the afternoon wore on, they found a bench with a breathtaking view of the island. Monica excused herself to use the bathroom, her heart light with the joy of the day.

"I'll be back in five minutes," she called over her shoulder.

"Be careful," Chandler replied, his voice laced with concern.

"I won't get lost," Monica reassured him, though she didn't know why she felt a sudden flutter of unease.

She wandered off, her thoughts wandering just as freely. As the minutes stretched on, she realized she had no idea where she was. She turned to retrace her steps, but Chandler was nowhere to be seen. Panic crept into her chest.

She tried calling him, but her phone was left with Chandler in the bag, forgotten. Desperation took hold as she searched for him, calling his name softly at first, then louder as the sun began to dip below the horizon.

"Where are you, Chandler?" she whispered to herself.

As she continued to search, her mind raced, memories of past heartbreak flooding back. Chandler had always been there for her, but now, she felt more alone than ever.

Meanwhile, Chandler was on his own frantic search, his worry growing with every passing minute. He remembered his past pain, the times he had lost someone he loved. The thought of losing Monica tore at him, and soon he was running through the paths they had walked together, calling out for her, his heart pounding.

When Monica finally returned to the spot where she had left him, she froze, her breath catching in her throat when she realized he was gone.

Then, she heard it: his voice, sharp and angry.

"You said you wouldn't get lost."

Monica turned around, and when she saw him, the floodgates opened. She rushed into his arms, crying uncontrollably.

"I was scared," she sobbed. "I kept walking, thinking of everything that could go wrong. But I don't want to lose you, Chandler. I love you."

A soft, relieved smile spread across Chandler's face. "I love you too," he whispered. "I'm so in love with you."

He opened his arms wide, and she fell into them, both of them holding each other as if nothing else mattered. They stood there, savoring the moment, the sunset casting a golden glow over the horizon. As night fell, they returned to the car, Monica's head resting against the window, the gentle motion of the car lulling her to sleep. Chandler glanced at her with a smile, his heart full.

"I didn't know it was this easy to make you happy," he said softly.

Monica stirred, murmuring a reply. "I am so happy."

Back in Calgary, Chandler drove Monica to her apartment. She leaned in, closing her eyes, ready to say goodnight, but Chandler paused. "I think maybe you should rest," he said, his voice gentle. "Sleep well, and have sweet dreams about me."

Monica smiled, warmth spreading through her. "Okay... you too."

As she walked away, she looked back at him, her heart light, but there was still something unspoken between them.

Later that night, Monica found herself wide awake, her mind racing. She tossed and turned, the events of the day replaying in her mind. Just as she was about to drift off, there was a knock at the door. She opened it to find Chandler standing there, breathless and sweating.

"Chandler? What's going on?" she asked.

"I couldn't stop thinking about you," he said, his voice thick with emotion. "Are you okay? Are you scared?"

Monica's eyes softened and a slow smile tugged at her lips. "Not anymore, Now that you're here." she whispered.

Without another word, Chandler stepped inside, closing the door behind him. The air between them shifted—charged with something deeper, something raw and magnetic.

Chandler reached for her, his hands cupping her face as he kissed her. Not a soft, tentative kiss, but one filled with everything they'd both been holding back—passion, longing, love.

Monica melted into him, her fingers threading through his hair, pulling him closer. Chandler's arms wrapped around her tightly, lifting her slightly off the ground before carrying her to the bedroom. The room was quiet except for their breathing, quick and shallow, hearts thudding in unison.

Chandler lay her down gently on the bed, never breaking eye contact. For a moment, they just looked at each other, breathless and smiling—an entire conversation passing between them in silence.

Then, slowly, his hands began to explore her body, reverent and warm, as if he were committing every curve to memory.

Monica reached for the buttons of his shirt, her touch trembling but certain. She slid it off his shoulders, revealing the lines of muscle beneath.

Then Monica kissed his collarbone, her lips brushing down his chest, and he let out a breath that trembled with restraint.

Clothes slipped away, one piece at a time, until there was nothing between them but skin and anticipation. The world outside faded. All that remained was this—his mouth on hers, her soft gasps filling the room, the way their bodies fit together like a long-lost puzzle finally made whole.

Chandler's touch was both tender and hungry, exploring her with a kind of wonder that made her heart ache. His lips traced along her jaw, down her neck, across her collarbone, lingering over the places that made her shiver.

Monica arched into him, whispering his name like a secret, over and over.

When he finally moved inside her, it was slow, reverent, as if they were writing a love letter with their bodies. They moved together in a rhythm that felt ancient, inevitable. Each moan, each kiss, each whispered word drew them closer, until neither of them could tell where one ended and the other began.

"I love you," Chandler whispered against her skin, again and again like a vow.

"I love you too," Monica breathed, her hands clutching at his back as they moved faster, caught in a wave of passion and heat.

They reached the edge together, clinging tightly, trembling with release. Afterward, they lay tangled in the sheets, their limbs entwined, foreheads pressed together, skin slick with sweat and hearts finally at peace.

Chandler kissed her gently. "You're everything," he murmured.

Monica smiled, her eyes heavy with sleep but filled with something brighter—hope. "Don't go," she whispered.

"I won't," he said. "Not tonight. Not ever."

Chapter 6

This Is What Love Looks Like

The soft light of morning filtered through the blinds, casting a gentle glow across the room. Chandler lay under the covers, asleep beside Monica, their bodies still tangled in a comfortable embrace.

Slowly, his eyelids fluttered open. He shifted slightly and glanced at her, watching as she slept soundly next to him. Her breath was slow and steady, her back rising and falling with each inhale. He couldn't help but smile at the peaceful sight.

The sound of a distant car engine hummed outside, typical for the bustling streets of downtown Calgary, but for a moment, everything felt still. Chandler shifted again, his body reluctantly leaving the warmth of the bed. He slipped out silently, careful not to disturb the fragile quiet.

Later, Monica stepped out of the shower, her wet hair cascading down her back, and dressed only in a loose shirt and underwear. She entered the kitchen to find Chandler standing at the stove, flipping an omelette with practiced ease. He caught her eye and gave a small smile.

"Good morning," he said, his voice warm.

Monica smiled back and walked over to the table, sitting down with a quiet sigh. "How can I help?"

Chandler shook his head. "No need. It's almost ready."

Monica didn't argue. Instead, she slipped her arms around him from behind, resting her head on his back. "I'm sure you could use the help."

Chandler chuckled. "Why so cute?"

Monica smiled against his back, the sound of his laughter sending a ripple of warmth through her chest.

"You make me greedy," she admitted, her voice barely above a whisper. "The more time I spend with you, the more I want you."

Chandler turned in her arms and gently took her hands in his. He lowered his voice, a touch of sincerity in his tone. "I want to hold you."

For a moment, they just stood there, hands intertwined, savoring the quiet closeness between them. Then Chandler lifted her into his arms and kissed her—long enough to forget the omelette still sizzling on the stove.

A sudden smell of burning snapped him back to reality. "The omelette!" he exclaimed, rushing to the stove just in time to rescue what was left.

Monica burst into laughter, but as she stepped forward, she slipped slightly on the smooth floor. Chandler caught her just in time, holding her tight. "I'm sorry," he said, breathless, brushing a damp strand of hair from her face. Then, with a grin, he scooped her up again and carried her to the table.

"Just sit here for a second, my queen. I'll bring you the best breakfast ever."

Monica laughed softly, but her heart fluttered at the affection shining in his eyes.

Chandler returned to the kitchen, this time more focused. A little while later, he reappeared with two plates, each carefully arranged—scrambled eggs, avocado slices, buttered toast, a mix of fresh fruit, and a light salad.

They sat together, sharing a quiet breakfast as morning light spilled through the window. Chandler watched her as she ate, a gentle smile playing on his lips.

Monica couldn't help but smile back at him. "Am I dreaming? Because if I am, I don't want to wake up," she said softly.

Chandler reached over and patted her head, a simple, affectionate gesture. Then, without a word, he reached into his pocket and pulled out a small jewelry box. Monica blinked, surprised. Her eyes widened as she took it from him and opened it. Inside was a pair of delicate, beautiful earrings.

She stared at them, stunned. But before she could say anything, Chandler leaned in and gently pulled her closer, his voice low and earnest.

"Let's live together," he said, his eyes searching hers. "You can move into my place, or I'll move into yours. Don't answer now. Take your time. I know it's fast, but if we don't want time to pass us by, we can't wait forever. I really love you."

Monica's heart pounded. She looked into his eyes, the warmth of his words settling deep inside her.

"I think it's destiny," she whispered. "I think it's destiny that brought us together—through all the silly little incidents."

"Is that a yes?" Chandler asked, a hopeful smile tugging at his lips.

"Yes," Monica replied, her smile widening. "Yes. Yes. Yes."

Chandler let out a joyful laugh and pulled her into a kiss, their connection deepening with each passing second.

They ended up on the bed, lying side by side, their fingers tracing the contours of each other's faces. Chandler buried his face in the curve of her neck, holding her close. For a long moment, they just stayed like that—wrapped up in each other, the world outside fading away.

As they shifted to find a more comfortable position, Chandler's eyes caught a small scar on her shoulder—a faint mark against her otherwise smooth skin. His fingers gently brushed over it, concern flickering in his gaze.

"What happened?" he asked softly.

Monica's eyes lowered, the memory surfacing like a shadow. "My dad did it... back when I tried to stop him from fighting with my mom."

Chandler's chest tightened at the words, his mind racing with thoughts of the man who had hurt her. He swallowed it down, focusing instead on the warmth of her skin beneath his fingertips.

"I'm so sorry," he breathed, the words soft and full of ache.

"It's alright," she said, her voice steady, though touched by sadness.

"It was a long time ago. I've mostly forgotten. But… there are more scars, Chandler. Things I haven't told you yet. Can I take my time to share them with you?"

Chandler nodded his voice gentle and full of understanding, "of course. Take all the time you need. We've got forever."

***

That evening, just outside the hair salon, Chandler waited in his car to pick Monica up for their dinner date.

Monica skipped down the steps, her hair catching the golden light, a soft smile playing on her lips. She hadn't felt this fluttery excitement in years.

Her coworkers waved her off with knowing smiles and lighthearted teasing. Their laughter faded as she climbed into Chandler's car. The drive was quiet, but comfortable—the kind of silence that spoke volumes.

They arrived at Bow Rivers Edge Campground, where Chandler had set up a cozy little tent beside a flickering campfire. Monica's eyes lit up as she took in the scene—a picnic blanket laid out, wine glasses ready, and soft music playing from a portable speaker.

The cool evening air brushed against their skin, carrying the fresh, earthy scent of pine and the crispness of the river nearby. The gentle sound of water flowing over rocks was a soothing backdrop to the crackling campfire, its warmth contrasting with the chill in the air.

Monica inhaled deeply, the scent of nature grounding her in the moment. The sky above deepened into a violet hue, stars starting to twinkle as the day's warmth began to slip away.

Chandler poured them both a glass of wine—the same kind he'd served the night they met at the bar.

"Don't worry, there are no peanuts this time," he joked, handing her the glass.

Monica laughed, clinking her glass gently against his. "Cheers."

"It's really nice to be here with you," Chandler said, his voice calm, content.

As the fire crackled and the sky faded into hues of violet and gold, Chandler turned more serious. "I have a question," he said, slightly hesitant. "What's your religion?"

Monica blinked, surprised. "Pardon?"

Chandler grinned, mischief in his eyes. "Because whatever it is… I need to know what you believe in to be that pretty."

Monica burst out laughing. "What?!"

They laughed together, the tension melting away. Then Chandler pulled out his phone and scrolled through photos from their recent city tour.

"You closed your eyes in almost every one," he said, amused.

"Do you ever take photos?" Chandler asked, tilting his head as he scrolled through more of their pictures.

Monica shrugged, a small smile tugging at her lips.

"Not really. I've always preferred being behind the camera. Or... not in the frame at all."

"Why?" he asked gently, genuinely curious.

She hesitated, her fingers curling around the stem of her glass. "I guess... growing up, I didn't like how I looked. And then later, I didn't like how I felt. It was easier not to capture those moments."

Chandler looked at her, his gaze soft but unwavering. "You're beautiful, Monica in every way. And the way I see you... I wish you could see it too."

Her eyes met his, something unspoken passing between them.

"I'm trying," she said quietly. "With you, it feels easier."

Chandler reached over, brushing his thumb across her cheek.

"One day, I'll fill a whole album with pictures of you smiling. Just wait."

Monica laughed her eyes misty but bright. "Only if I get to take some of you, too," she insisted.

"Deal," he said, raising his glass.

They clinked glasses again, the firelight dancing in their eyes. Then, with a playful glint, Chandler tapped his phone and a soft, romantic song began to drift through the speaker—slow, melodic, full of unspoken promises.

He stood and extended his hand toward her.

"Dance with me," he said gently.

Monica laughed softly, shaking her head. "I can't."

"Yes, you can," Chandler insisted, his voice low, coaxing. "Just follow me."

She hesitated for a moment, her fingers nervously brushing the rim of her glass. But then she looked up at him—really looked—and saw the warmth, the patience in his outstretched hand.

With a breath, she rose and slipped her hand into his.

They moved slowly, swaying in rhythm with the music and the crackling fire. The world around them blurred—the scent of pine, the hush of the river, the golden flicker of flames—all fading into the background as they held each other close.

The night wrapped gently around them like a promise.

Chapter 7

The Proposal That Almost Was

A year had passed since Monica moved in with Chandler. Now, they found themselves in the kitchen, the oven humming softly and the faint scent of smoke curling through the atmosphere as Monica attempted to bake a cake from scratch—her second try that morning.

Chandler peeked into the oven with a teasing grin. "Is this one supposed to look like a volcano, or...?"

Monica tossed a dish towel at him with a laugh. "Go sit down before I throw flour at you."

Just then, the doorbell rang. Monica wiped her hands on her apron and hurried to answer it. When she opened the door, Irena and her husband stood there with a bright smile and a bottle of wine in hand.

"Welcome! Where are the kids?" Monica asked, pulling her into a warm hug.

"They're at home, don't worry. Nanny's got them," Irena replied with a laugh, stepping inside.

As Monica entered the kitchen with Irena, she saw Chandler standing by the stove, a small smile playing on his lips.

"Hi, Chandler," Irena greeted him.

"Hi," Chandler said, nodding in return. "Guess I'll just keep your husband company."

He quickly excused himself and left the room, and Irena turned to Monica, her expression curious.

"What's with the cooking?" she teased. "We could just go out and buy food."

Monica paused, glancing down at the cake she was struggling to bake. "I used to bake," she said. "But I probably should've checked the recipe online."

Irena asked. "Are you trying to impress him? Bake him a cake?"

Monica smiled softly, her eyes glinting with affection. "I love him, I really do. It's been a year since we started living together, and… it's still a little awkward, but I wouldn't change a thing. He's easy-going, gets along with everyone."

Irena studied her for a moment then nodded approvingly. "I can see the changes in you, the good kind. You two… you're a good match."

Monica's heart fluttered at her friend's words, and Irena pulled her into a hug. "Just enjoy it. Be happy. You deserve it."

As the evening wound down and Irena and her husband filtered out, Monica and Chandler were left alone. Monica clasped his hand tightly, a smile curving her lips.

"I think we've got a good thing going," she whispered, her heart full.

Chandler grinned. "I think so too."

Monica handed Chandler a small bracelet, her fingers brushing his as she placed it in his palm.

"Wear this bracelet," she said, her voice soft but full of meaning.

"Did you make this?" Chandler asked, surprised.

Monica nodded, her eyes shining. "It's a matching set for us. These bracelets will bring us luck," she said.

Chandler held it close, his heart full. "Thank you, Monica. You make me feel like I'm shining bright every day."

***

The soft, flickering glow of candlelight bathed the table, casting delicate shadows on the elegant decor. Monica and Chandler sat in a cozy corner of one of Calgary's most renowned restaurants, enjoying a quiet dinner.

The sound of conversation from nearby tables blended with the soothing background music, creating a perfect atmosphere for a special evening.

Monica took a bite of her meal, savoring the rich flavors as she looked across the table at Chandler.

"This is delicious," she said, her smile warm and appreciative.

Chandler's face brightened and he asked enthusiastically, "really? That's good to hear."

Chandler hand trembled slightly as he reached into his jacket pocket. He fumbled with a small velvet box, pulling it out with a nervous breath.

"Do... Do...," he muttered to himself, trying to steady his nerves.

Monica glanced at him, a bit confused by his sudden unease. "Chandler, what's wrong?"

But before he could respond, his shaking hand fumbled, and the small box slipped from his grip. In his frantic attempt to catch it, he knocked over one of the candles, sending a flicker of fire toward the tablecloth. The flames caught quickly, and panic surged through Chandler.

"No, no, no!" he shouted, scrambling for the fire extinguisher. He grabbed it from the wall and sprayed foam all around, covering not just the fire, but also Monica, who sat frozen in shock.

"I'm so sorry! I didn't mean to—" Chandler stammered, trying to wipe foam from Monica's face as she sat there, blinking in disbelief.

Monica stared at him, trying not to laugh. Despite the chaos, the humor of the moment wasn't lost on her.

***

A short while later, Chandler sat with Anna and Sophia at a nearby cafe bar, nursing a drink to calm his nerves. Both women were trying to contain their laughter, clearly enjoying the absurdity of the situation.

"That happened, and you two are laughing?" Chandler groaned. "It's not funny! I need your help, seriously!"

Anna and Sophia exchanged amused glances before bursting into another round of laughter.

"It was kind of funny, though," Anna said between chuckles.

"Honestly, it was classic," Sophia added, wiping away a tear of laughter.

Chandler slouched in his chair, defeated. "I can't believe that just happened. Tomorrow, when I lifts my hand like this," Chandler said, holding his hand in the air, "Sophia, that's your signal to bring out the bouquet. And I'll do the rest."

Chandler took a deep breath, pulled the ring out of his pocket, showing it to them with a nervous smile.

Chandler started playing gesture his fingers like he was playing piano. "And Anna, when I do like this with my hands, you start playing her favorite song."

He looked at them both, his face full of anxiety.

"Please, let's not mess this up," he added, almost pleading.

***

The next evening, Chandler and Monica were seated at a cozy corner table in a fancy restaurant once again.

Chandler was pacing nervously near the staircase, his mind racing. He glanced at Anna and Sophia, who were standing by the railing, waiting for their cue.

Chandler approached Monica, who was still sitting at the table, waiting patiently. He felt the pressure mounting in his chest, but he tried to act casual.

"Sorry to keep you waiting," Chandler said, trying to sound calm. "There was a long line at the restroom."

Monica smiled, brushing a stray lock of hair from her face. "It's alright. This place is beautiful, though. I'm just glad we're finally here."

A waitress arrived at the table, delivering the menus and taking their food order. After she left, Chandler sighed in relief. "The ambiance here is amazing," he said, trying to steer the conversation back to normal.

Monica nodded, her eyes scanning the view through the large windows, which overlooked the twinkling lights of downtown Calgary. She smiled, admiring the sight. "I love the view from here. If anyone proposes here, they're sure to succeed."

Chandler's heart skipped a beat, and he couldn't help but think that this might be the moment.

"Do you think so?" he asked, his voice a little too eager.

Monica continued to gaze out the window, and Chandler took a quick glance toward Anna and Sophia, who were waiting for the signal.

"Yeah, but..." Monica paused, her expression shifting. "Honestly, I'd hate it."

Chandler blinked, confused. "What? Why?"

Monica turned to face him, her smile fading slightly. "I mean, it's one thing to watch someone else get proposed to, but if that ever happened to me, I'd be so embarrassed. People would be watching me, and that would just... give me chills. It's not my type."

Chandler felt his stomach drop. This isn't happening. "Is that so?" he asked, trying to recover.

Monica nodded, her gaze softening. "Yes. I think most women actually want something more private, something personal. Not in a public place like this."

Chandler sighed under his breath. This is bad. He quickly glanced toward Anna and Sophia, who were standing by the staircase with flowers in hand, waiting for his cue. He subtly shook his head and waved them off.

"You're right," Chandler said, turning back to Monica. "Honestly, I'd never imagine proposing in a place like this either."

Then, under his breath, he muttered toward the staircase, "Don't do it."

Monica raised a brow. "What?"

Anna and Sophia exchanged confused glances.

"Did he just tell us to stop?" Anna asked.

"I don't know," Sophia replied. "Everything's ready!"

Anna hesitated. "Should we...?"

Sophia sighed. "Let's just go. We're already here."

The two of them slowly started down the staircase, bouquet of flowers in hand.

Chandler spotted them out of the corner of his eye and panicked.

"Look!" Chandler suddenly shouted, pointing wildly out the window. "Bear!"

Monica startled, turning to look. "What? Where?"

Seizing the moment, Chandler dashed over to Anna and Sophia. "Abort the plan! Abort!" he hissed. "Go hide, now!"

Monica turned back to the table, blinking. "Wait... where did he go?"

Chandler ducked behind the staircase with Anna and Sophia.

"Change of plans," he whispered. "We're postponing. She literally just said she'd hate a public proposal."

"But everything's ready!" Anna protested.

"I know," Chandler sighed. "But I'm not doing this if it's not what she wants. I'll figure out something better. Later."

Without waiting for another word, Chandler straightened his jacket, took a deep breath, and hurried back to the table just as the waitress arrived with their meals. He slid into his seat, forcing a smile.

The rest of the dinner passed quietly, the candlelight flickering between them. Both lost in their thoughts, neither of them knowing that something even better was waiting just around the corner.

***

Later, back at the cafe, Sophia, Anna, and Chandler sat around, trying to laugh off the chaos of the night. Irena joined them, unable to hold back her amusement.

"I can't believe this just happened," Chandler groaned, still in disbelief.

Irena tried to stifle her laughter but couldn't help herself. "I'm not laughing... well, maybe just a little."

"Okay, okay, it was funny," Irena said, grinning. "But seriously, I've got a new plan. This time, it's foolproof."

Monica finished up her work at the salon and checked her phone, reading Chandler's text.

CHANDLER (TEXT) I'm busy tonight, will come home late. Enjoy your dinner. Love you.

She tucked her phone away and stepped out of the salon, where Irena was waiting for her.

"Wait one minute," Monica said, pausing in the doorway. "I'll be right back."

Irena asked. "Where's Chandler?"

"He's busy at the hospital. Looks like it's just us tonight," Monica said.

Meanwhile, the cafe had been transformed. Anna, Sophia, and Chandler had decorated it with flowers, petals, and twinkling lights, all carefully arranged for Monica's surprise.

Chandler looked around at the scene, his hands trembling in anticipation. His heart raced as he practiced the words he was about to say.

"Thank you, Monica, for coming into my life," he muttered to himself. "I want to be with you, in both the good times and the bad. Could I do that? I love you, Monica. Will you marry me?"

As he said the words aloud for the first time, he felt a surge of emotion. But when he reached into his pocket to pull out the ring, his hand came up empty.

"Shit," Chandler muttered his face paling. "I forgot the ring at home."

Chandler's car sped away from the cafe, its tires slipping slightly on the slick, icy roads of Calgary.

At the same time, Monica's car drew closer completely unaware of the chaos Chandler had just left in his wake.

Monica's car rolled to a stop outside the café.

The windows glowed warmly against the chill of the evening, strings of tiny lights twinkling above the entrance. Her breath fogged the glass as she exhaled, a soft, tired smile pulling at her lips. It's good of Irena to pull me out tonight, she thought. I needed this. But as her hand reached for the door handle an odd weight settled in her chest.

A sudden, inexplicable sense of absence, as if something important had been misplaced somewhere out of reach. The sensation clung to her like a second skin, brittle and cold. She hesitated.

Inside, Anna and Sophia exchanged uneasy glances. The decorations were still in place from earlier in the week, petals scattered like small, careless promises across the table. The bouquet in the center drooped slightly, its leaves wilting in the warm air.

"Should we call him?" Sophia murmured, her fingers trailing the rim of her coffee cup.

"He'll be back," Anna said, but even she didn't believe it.

***

Ten days later, the tension lingered like a storm cloud refusing to break.

Monica paced the living room, the phone pressed against her ear, listening to the empty ring before the screen flashed Call Failed for the fourth time that morning. A sharp sigh escaped her as she let her hand drop, raking restless fingers through her hair.

Irena sat curled on the couch, watching her quietly. The air between them felt too still, the silence thick and unyielding.

"Still nothing?" Irena asked.

Monica shook her head. The knot in her stomach tightened with each passing hour. "His phone's off. It's been days, Irena. No one's seen him. No one's heard a word."

She sank onto the couch beside Irena, burying her face in her hands.

"I don't like this feeling," Monica whispered. "It's not like him."

Irena hesitated then reached out, squeezing her friend's hand. "Maybe it's not what you think. Let's… let's call Michael."

Monica hesitated then nodded. She picked up the phone again, fingers trembling as she found Michael's number. It rang twice before he picked up.

"Hello, Monica."

His voice was steady.

"Where the hell is Chandler?" she demanded, the words tumbling out rough and desperate. "Why is his phone off? No one's seen him, Michael. It's been ten days."

A pause then came the reply. Smooth, "I told you — he's in Africa at a camp."

"Africa?" Monica's brow furrowed. "What kind of camp doesn't allow phones or… any contact? And you're telling me no one can reach him? No messages. No updates?"

"I'm sure there's a reason," Michael said. "Look, don't stress. He'll be back in a few days. And hey — why don't you come by the hospital for a check-up?"

"What? Why?"

"Nothing serious," he added, too quickly, "routine stuff."

Before she could reply, Michael disconnect the call. Monica stared at the phone in her hand, numb. The apartment felt colder somehow, the walls closer. A leaden certainty settled over her.

Something was wrong. She could feel it in her bones.

Michael slipped his phone into his pocket as he made his way down the corridor. The hospital was quieter than usual, the fluorescent lights casting long reflections on the polished floors. He moved with practiced ease, but his expression was tight, his thoughts elsewhere.

As he turned the corner, he nearly collided with Chandler.

Chandler was mid-sentence, a faint grin tugging at his lips. Beside him stood Rachel — tall, striking, and with the kind of easy familiarity that made Michael's stomach tighten. The way she stood a little too close, the way Chandler's hand brushed her arm as he spoke — it told a story without needing words.

Their conversation faltered as Michael approached.

"Hey," Chandler greeted, a little too casual, as if nothing in the world was wrong.

Michael's eyes flicked to Rachel, then back to Chandler. "I need a word."

Something in his tone made Chandler's smile falter.

Rachel, sensing the shift, offered a polite nod. "I'll catch you later."

As she walked away, her heels clicking softly against the linoleum, Michael watched her go before turning back to Chandler.

"You've got people looking for you," he said quietly. "Ten days, man you planning on answering your phone anytime soon? Monica's tearing herself apart."

A flicker of something crossed Chandler's face.

Without waiting for a reply, Michael moved past him, leaving Chandler standing alone in the corridor

The ring Monica hadn't yet seen rested safely in Chandler's pocket. He toyed with it absently as they spoke.

Chapter 8

When the Rain Fell Hardest

Monica, accompanied by Irena, walked toward Michael's hospital room. As they passed through the hallway, Chandler and Rachel exited together, their voices low and intimate. Neither Monica nor Irena noticed them.

Later, outside the hospital, Irena turned to Monica.

"I'll run inside to grab the medicine. You can bring the car around."

Monica nodded, distracted by her racing thoughts. As Irena headed toward the pharmacy, she glanced back—and froze.

Standing by the hospital's side entrance were Chandler and Rachel, talking. Their faces were close, their conversation intense. A chill crept down Irena's spine.

No... it can't be, she thought, shaken.

On the drive home, Irena's anxiety was palpable. She kept glancing at Monica, hesitant to speak.

"Any news from Chandler?" she asked casually.

"He'll be back in a couple of days," Monica replied, trying to sound lighthearted.

Irena hesitated. "I might be wrong… but I think I saw him at the hospital with some woman."

Monica shook her head firmly. "You're mistaken."

That night, Monica sat on the edge of her bed, obsessively checking her phone, still no messages. No missed calls. She stared at a photo of the two of them, her thumb tracing Chandler's face.

"You're the only person I can lean on in this world," she whispered, her voice breaking. Why aren't you here?

She lingered there, lost in memories, until exhaustion overtook her.

The next morning, sunlight streamed through the curtains. Monica jolted awake and grabbed her phone. A message from Chandler flashed across the screen:

CHANDLER TEXT: We need to meet today. Come to the hospital. I want to tell you something.

Her heart pounded. Was this the moment she'd been waiting for?

At the hospital, Chandler waited outside. Monica's heart leapt when she saw him, and she rushed into his arms. But he stiffened, pulling away slightly.

"Did I scare you?" Monica laughed nervously. "Sorry—I was just… excited."

Chandler's face was unreadable. "Come inside," he said quietly. "There's something I need to say."

As they turned toward the entrance, a sudden downpour began. And then—Rachel appeared, approaching Chandler with a soft smile before wrapping her arms around him.

Monica's feet felt rooted to the ground, her heart pounding in her chest. She stared at Chandler, her breath catching in her throat, before her eyes flicked to the woman beside him. A cold emptiness settled over her.

"You..." She swallowed, her voice trembling. "Who is she?"

"I'm his fiancée," Rachel replied smoothly.

Monica's breath hitched. "You're joking, right?" She turned to Chandler, desperate for denial. "Tell me this isn't true. Tell me you didn't... you wouldn't cheat. Not you."

Chandler's face softened for a moment. "I'm sorry for showing you this side of me... but this is who I am."

Monica's sobs erupted as she turned and ran into the rain. Chandler chased after her.

"Monica—wait!"

She spun around, striking his chest with clenched fists.

"How could you do this? Were you always this cruel?"

The rain slowed, a somber hush falling over them.

"I'm sorry," Chandler whispered.

That evening, Monica stood on her balcony, staring up at the indifferent moon. The ache inside her chest was unbearable. Every memory of Chandler—the way he looked at her, the times he made her laugh without trying, the way he made her feel safe—all of it felt like a cruel betrayal now.

Meanwhile, Chandler lay in a hospital bed, drained and pale. Michael sat beside him.

"You okay?" Michael asked, though his voice said he already knew the answer.

"I'm fine," Chandler murmured.

Michael hesitated. "Why not tell Monica the truth? Is it worth all this pain?"

Chandler stared at the ceiling. "How can I? I love her... so much. But I can't drag her into this. It's better this way."

Michael shook his head. "You're wrong. The longer you lie, the deeper her wounds will be."

Moments later, Chandler lost in his thoughts. Michael returned, breathless.

"Monica's here. She insists on seeing you."

Chandler's heart clenched.

"I'll handle it," he said quietly, donning his doctor's coat.

In his office, sunlight cut through the blinds in thin stripes. Monica stepped in, pale but resolute. Neither spoke at first. The air was thick with unspoken things.

"What do you want, Monica?" Chandler asked at last.

She swallowed hard, taking a careful step closer.

"I don't believe what you said about you and Rachel. I don't buy it. Not a word."

Chandler's gaze hardened. "I don't care what you believe. Remember when you once said no one ever stays forever? That in the end, we're all alone."

Monica's face crumpled. "How foolish I was... to expect anything else from you."

Chandler's voice was cold. "It's only been a year. If you can't get over that…"

Monica stood tall, wiping her tears. "You don't have to be so cruel."

She left without another word.

***

A few weeks later, Monica sat in a café, tears streaming down her face. Anna, Sophia, and Irena gathered around her.

"Irena's voice was soft but firm. "Monica, why are you crying?"

Monica's chest tightened, a sob lodged in her throat. "I don't know anymore. The tears just keep coming, and I don't know how to stop them."

Irena shook her head, a quiet frustration in her eyes. "Your life isn't over, Monica. You have to show him that. You have to live with dignity. Don't let him see you broken."

Anna, always the realist, leaned in, her tone soft but insistent. "Think about your baby. You can't keep doing this. The stress, the tears… it's not good for you. You have to keep going."

Monica's hands trembled as she wiped away the tears, her fingers brushing her stomach instinctively. "I know. I know I have to keep going. But every time I try to forget him, I remember… and it hurts. I can't stop the pain. And I don't want this... I don't want my baby to feel this, too."

Later that night, Anna lay beside her as Monica stirred restlessly.

"Hand me the phone," Monica whispered. "I want to call him."

"No way," Anna replied firmly.

Monica's voice turned bitter. "You're right. Why should I? Let him be happy with his new fiancée."

Then, after a long silence:

"Just once. I need to hear his voice."

"No," Anna said again.

Back at the hospital, Chandler winced as a needle pierced his skin. Rachel held his hand, but his gaze was distant.

***

Months earlier, on the night he planned to propose, Chandler's world had shifted. He received a call from his step mother.

STEP-MOTHER (phone call, crying): "Your father had a heart attack…"

Chandler pulled up to his father's house, his car coming to a slow stop in the driveway.

The ride had been long and silent, filled with the kind of heaviness that only bad news could bring. His mind raced, but there was nothing to focus on except the dread growing in his chest.

Chandler sat in the car for a moment, staring at the front door, before forcing himself to open the car's door and step out.

The rain had started to fall, a gentle drizzle at first, but it quickly turned into a downpour, soaking through his jacket. He stood there for a moment, collecting himself before walking up to the front door and ringing the bell. His stepmother opened it almost immediately, her eyes swollen from crying.

"Chandler..." she said, her voice trembling.

"How is he?" Chandler asked his throat tight.

"Come inside," she replied softly, stepping aside. "The doctor says it was a minor heart attack. He'll be fine in a couple of days, but we have to be careful."

Chandler nodded numbly and stepped into the house, following her to his father's room.

Minutes passed before Chandler's father stirred, his eyes blinking open. He looked around, disoriented, and then focused on Chandler. He lifted a weak arm and pulled his son into a hug.

Chandler, still sobbing, held him tightly, as if afraid that if he let go, his father might slip away.

But then Chandler froze. Through his tears, he saw her—Rachel—standing in the doorway. Her face was a mixture of guilt and sadness, and Chandler's heart lurched. It had been years since he had seen her, years since he had thought of her. His emotions were a tangle of confusion, anger, and hurt.

Soon Chandler went left his father house. He stood frozen in place, his legs unwilling to carry him.

The storm outside seemed to mirror his inner turmoil as the rain came down in sheets.

Rachael stepped outside her footsteps soft on the wet ground. Chandler turned to her, voice hoarse with emotion, his heart racing.

"What are you doing here?" he asked.

But before Rachael could respond to Chandler.

"No," Chandler muttered, his breath coming in shallow gasps.

"No, you can't just show up here after all this time. You left me. You left without a word, without a trace. And now you're here? For the last ten years, I've been a mess because of you. I couldn't forget you. And finally, after everything, when I thought I could move on... when I found peace... you show up."

Rachel didn't answer at first. She just looked at him, her gaze full of regret. Finally, she spoke, her voice quiet, almost apologetic.

"I'm here as your father's doctor," she said softly.

Chandler tried to move, but stumbled, his foot catching on the wet pavement, and he fell to the ground with a grunt. His hands and knees scraped against the concrete, but he barely noticed the pain.

Rachael stepped forward, reaching out to him, her hand extended in a gesture of support. But Chandler didn't take her hand. With a strained breath, Chandler pushed himself to his feet, his body trembling slightly from the effort, ignoring the sting of the wounds on his palms and knees, and made his way toward his car, as if escaping the world around him would ease the ache in his heart.

Chandler finally made it back to his building, his steps slow and heavy.

The weight of everything—his father's health, his unresolved feelings for Rachel, the years of pain he had tried to bury—crushed him, leaving him breathless.

Michael was waiting outside the building, leaning against the wall. When he saw Chandler, he stood up straight, concern flashing across his face.

"Where the hell have you been?" Michael asked his voice sharp. "Did you go to heaven to get the ring?"

Chandler didn't respond. He could barely keep his eyes open, his body trembling from the emotional and physical strain. Without warning, his legs gave way, and his vision blurred. His body collapsed to the ground, and everything went black.

***

Chandler awoke in a hospital bed days later. Blurry. Disoriented.

"Where am I?"

Rachel answered quietly. "You collapsed. We ran tests."

"What's wrong with me?"

Rachel hesitated then looked to Michael. "The MRI showed a tumor. It's brain cancer. Stage three."

Chandler's world stopped.

"Is this a joke?"

"No," Rachel said, her voice trembling, the words barely escaping her lips.

She paused for a moment, looking down at the chart in her hands as if unwilling to meet Chandler's gaze.

"It's already over 4 cm… the prognosis isn't good."

The words hit him like a physical blow. Chandler opened his mouth to speak, but nothing came out. His face crumpled with pain and shock, his entire being numb—as if the world around him was collapsing.

"Can I talk to you alone for a moment?" he asked Michael, his voice barely holding together.

Rachel stepped out, leaving the two men alone in the room.

Chandler's voice cracked when he spoke. "What should I do? My father… Monica… I have people to take care of."

Michael's heart twisted at the sight of his friend so broken. "You have to tell them," he said quietly, his voice gentle but steady.

Chandler looked away, his throat tightening. "Do you think she can handle it?"

"We won't know until you tell her," Michael replied softly.

A deep sigh escaped Chandler's lips, his expression hollow.

"Maybe breaking up with Monica is the best choice."

Michael's brow furrowed. "Why are you talking like this?"

Chandler's voice cracked, his hands clenched into fists at his sides. "Love… it's supposed to make you feel alive, right? But all it's doing is dragging us both down. I'll be the one to hurt her. I'll be the one who causes her pain. And that's what terrifies me most."

His eyes squeezed shut, the weight of his own words almost too much to bear. "I'll hurt her, Michael. I'll tear her apart, and I don't know if I can live with that."

***

Later, in the hospital cafeteria, Michael and Rachel sat across from each other, quietly sipping their tea.

"It's his decision," Rachel said softly, her voice heavy with resignation. "He's decided not to tell anyone. At least… not for now."

Back in his hospital room, Rachel reentered quietly, her gaze searching Chandler's face as he sat up in bed.

"How are you feeling now?" she asked her voice gentler this time.

"Better," Chandler replied, forcing a faint smile. "You don't have to worry."

"I have to. I'm your doctor," she said, a firm kindness in her tone.

There was a pause. She seemed to gather her thoughts, took a slow step closer. Her voice lowered, touched with regret. "I'm sorry. I really am. I gave you such deep wounds."

Silence hung between them before Chandler finally spoke, his voice thick with emotion. "I need a favor."

Rachel surprised. "What is it?"

Chandler met her gaze, his eyes vulnerable and desperate. "Will you pretend to be my fiancée?"

Chapter 9

By Your Side, No Matter What

Back in the present, Chandler lay in his hospital bed, hooked up to monitors and IV drips. The steady beep of the heart monitor filled the otherwise silent room. His eyes remained closed, his body too weak to move, but his mind restless. Rachel sat by his side, holding his hand, offering what little comfort she could. She watched the rise and fall of his chest, silently willing him to fight.

The next week, fate intervened in its quiet, unrelenting way.

Chandler and Monica unexpectedly found themselves face to face at a small, quiet restaurant downtown. Neither of them had expected to run into the other, and for a brief moment, time seemed to stall around them.

Chandler's heart skipped as he took her in. She looked different — a softness around her face, a slight fullness he hadn't noticed before. He wondered, his mind foolishly jumping to the conclusion that maybe the weight came from heartbreak, the aftermath of their messy ending. He didn't know the truth she carried quietly within her.

At the same time, Monica's gaze swept over Chandler, noting the paleness of his face, the hollowness beneath his eyes. There was something different about him too. Something fragile, something she couldn't quite place. Unaware of the sickness weighing him down, she felt a pang of unease in her chest.

Both of them wore their wounds well, hidden beneath the polite smiles and wary glances, as if neither was ready to confront the ghosts still hanging between them.

"If you're destined to meet, you're bound to meet," Chandler thought to himself, a wry twist to the words. "No matter how hard you try to avoid them."

Later, outside the restaurant, Chandler walked. Monica followed him, then she confront him, her voice soft but insistent. "I'm sure you're a very good fiancée. Does she make you laugh? Does she ever make you cry or cause you heartache... not even once?"

"Yes, I'm very happy with her," Chandler replied, his voice tight, not meeting her gaze.

"Then why are you eating alone here?" Monica asked her voice full of quiet confusion. "I know you're not happy."

Monica's voice wavered with a question that had been on her mind. "One thing I don't understand—how can love change in an instant?"

"That's right," Chandler said his voice low and heavy. "Love doesn't change slowly. It changes in one moment. At first, you don't realize it. Then you pretend it hasn't changed. You try so hard until it finally comes to an end."

He paused, and his face softened as he spoke the words he had been avoiding. "I don't know when that one moment happened, but I do know that the end has come. Let's stop this."

Monica's eyes filled with tears, and she cried out.

"I wish you happiness," Chandler continued, his voice thick with emotion. "Don't look at your past, but look forward."

Chandler turned to walk away, but Monica grabbed his hand, refusing to let go. Chandler turned to face her, his heart breaking.

"Don't follow me," he said, his voice a sharp command, though his own tears betrayed him.

Monica, unable to stop herself, took a few more steps. Finally, Chandler snapped. His voice, filled with frustration, echoed in the quiet night.

"Are you a fool?" he yelled, tears streaming down his face. "I told you not to come."

He sobbed, his body shaking, but he forced himself to turn away, knowing it was the right thing to do. His footsteps were heavy as he moved forward, but the pain in his heart was unbearable. Monica followed a few more steps before he collapsed, clutching his abdomen.

"What's wrong?" Monica asked in a panic, rushing to his side.

"Nothing," Chandler muttered, trying to push her away.

But his legs gave out, and he stumbled again, unable to control his body.

Monica drove Chandler to the hospital, staying by his side as he was admitted. She watched anxiously as nurses and doctors surrounded him.

"Are you with this patient?" a nurse asked, her tone cold but professional.

Chandler, in agony, managed to summon enough strength to speak.

"No, she's not. She's not," he said, his voice weak but insistent.

"Go away," he added, his words sharp, though they cut Monica to the core.

Michael rushed into the room, taking charge of the situation. Chandler, desperate, called out to him.

"Michael... I'm scared."

In the hospital waiting room, Monica sat in silence, her eyes fixed on the door. Michael eventually emerged, his expression soft but serious.

"Don't worry," he said. "He's okay now."

Monica's heart raced. "What just happened? What's going on here?"

Michael sighed, sitting beside her. He explained everything—the diagnosis, the surgery, the complications that had followed. Monica's eyes filled with tears as she listened, her heart breaking for the man she still loved. Monica, dressed in the same clothes as the day before, sat by Chandler's bed. She had dozed off, but the sound of movement woke her. Chandler stirred beside her, his eyes fluttering open.

"Are you okay?" Monica asked her voice full of concern.

Chandler nodded faintly. "I am better... just felling sleepy."

Later that night, Chandler awoke to find Monica still holding his hand. His voice, weak and pained, broke the silence.

"Why are you here?" he asked, his eyes searching hers for answers.

"Look me in the eyes," Monica said, her voice gentle but insistent. "Tell me that you didn't miss me at all, and that I mean nothing to you."

Chandler turned his gaze away, his throat tight.

"I don't have the right to love anyone," he replied, his words carrying the weight of his fear and guilt.

Monica's face softening with understanding. "Why do you need a right to love?"

She reached for him, her eyes locked on his. "No matter what happens, I won't let you be alone, even when you're hurt."

She leaned in slowly, her lips brushing his. Chandler stayed still, tears streaming down his cheeks. His heart ached as he spoke again, his voice full of fear.

"This disease isn't a joke," he said hoarsely. "There's a chance I could die during surgery... or become paralyzed. Or before surgery, during chemo, I'll change physically and mentally. With a ticking time bomb inside me, how could I ask you to stay with me?"

"Why?" Monica asked, her voice breaking with emotion. "It doesn't matter to me. If I were like this, would you just abandon me and run away?"

"No. Never," Chandler replied without hesitation.

Monica's face softened, her eyes searching his as she held his hand tightly. "See? You would do that too. Why are you telling me I can't? Do you think I can just abandon you?"

She placed both hands on his and with resolute voice.

"Chandler... just like I am precious to you, you are precious to me. So stop pushing me away. There's no use now. Even if you push me away, I'm not going to budge."

Silence hung in the air between them before Chandler finally looked up, his heart full of emotion. Slowly, he pulled her into a tight embrace.

"I should have told you sooner," he whispered.

***

At the hospital, Irena, Sophia, and Anna visited Chandler, who was recovering in his room. There was a lingering sadness in the air. They hadn't known about his illness until it was nearly too late. But now, seeing him alive, they were filled with relief.

Each of them gave Chandler a hug, offering words of encouragement.

Chandler took their hands, holding them gently. His gratitude was clear, though he didn't speak. Instead, his eyes welled up with silent tears. The women left, giving Monica and Chandler some time alone.

Monica stepped closer. Chandler, his arm already reaching out, pulled her close and draped it around her.

"I am so grateful that you're here with me now," he whispered, his voice thick with emotion.

Later that evening, Chandler was filled with nervous anticipation as he prepared for chemotherapy. The thought of what was to come unsettled him, but there was also a strange calm in the air. He and Monica had agreed to cut his hair, a small ritual to take control of the situation in whatever way they could.

"This is good timing," Chandler said, a smile tugging at his lips. "I've always wanted you to cut my hair. I think the universe brought us together for this."

Tears began to stream down Chandler's face as Monica carefully worked with the clippers, cutting his hair down to a simple burr cut, or perhaps closer to a bald look.

Chandler closed his eyes, feeling the vibration of the clippers against his scalp. He didn't open them until Monica was finished. When he finally did, he looked at his new, much shorter hairstyle.

His hand reached for hers. He grasped it tightly, a silent thank you in his eyes. A few moments later, Monica returned with a cup of tea, handing it to him.

"I don't want to make your life uncomfortable," Chandler said his voice low.

Monica smiled softly, setting the tea aside. "I admit, life will be difficult. But you know, I love you even more now. I feel sympathy for you, and that makes me love you deeper."

Chandler's smile faltered for a moment. Monica saw it and asked gently, "You don't like hearing that, do you?"

He smiled again, the tension easing. "Love, plus sympathy, is just adding more love to the love."

Monica moved closer, kneeling beside him. "Thank you for coming into my life. I know there will be so much hardship ahead, but instead of being by your side only when you're happy, I want to be with you through the hard times. I want to share your burden. Will you marry us? We are not taking 'no' for an answer."

Chandler frowned in confusion. "'We'?"

Monica's lips curved into a tender smile as she reached for his hand and placed it on her stomach. "Surprise," she whispered. "You're not just marrying me… you're going to be a father."

For a moment, Chandler's world tilted. His heart skipped a beat as his eyes darted between hers and the hand beneath his palm. His throat tightened emotion too thick to speak.

Chandler's heart skipped a beat as he took her hand. "Yes. I will marry you. I love you. I'm in love with you."

"I know," Monica replied, her voice full of certainty.

They kissed, a gentle moment of shared relief, before they were interrupted by the phone ringing. The unexpected distraction made them laugh easing the weight of the moment.

Chapter 10
Walking Down the Aisle of Time

The next day, Monica stood outside the operating room, watching as Chandler was wheeled in. She felt the sting of fear in her chest, but there was also hope. The bouquet of flowers she had brought with her felt like a symbol of everything they still had to fight for.

A few weeks later, Irena, Sophia, Anna, and Monica were at a lingerie shop. The mood was light, a rare moment of normalcy in the midst of everything else.

Anna held up a set of lingerie with a knowing grin. "What do you think?" she asked Monica.

Monica looked at the set and laughed. "That's too much."

Sophia chimed in, showing Monica a simpler option. "How about this one?"

Irena, ever the mischief-maker, held up a lacy number with buttons down the front. "What about this? I'm sure Chandler will love this one."

Anna added with a laugh, "Chandler will run out of breath trying to unbutton that.

Meanwhile, Chandler, looking a little healthier, made his way to Michael's room at the hospital. He had a slight limp from the surgery, but his determination was evident.

"Don't worry," Michael said, as he glanced over Chandler's charts. "Your recovery from surgery is on track. The pain you're feeling is probably from the stress of the wedding preparation, but remember, surgery is just one part of your treatment. You still need to continue with chemotherapy. Make sure you eat properly and take your meds."

Chandler glanced down at the prescription Michael had given him. He noticed it was for painkillers, not digestive aids. Something didn't feel right, but he wasn't ready to face that yet.

Monica arrived at Michael's office just as Chandler was leaving. They missed each other by mere moments.

"Chandler's relief until now must have been a placebo effect," Michael said bluntly, his eyes flicking over to Monica. "He thought the surgery worked, but it hasn't."

Monica's heart dropped into her stomach. "What do you mean?"

Michael sighed. "Chandler will figure it out soon enough. But I've kept this from him because I promised you I would. It's not the time to tell him yet."

Monica nodded, her voice shaking. "Please, Michael, keep this secret just a little longer. At least until after the wedding. I don't know how Chandler will handle this if he finds out now."

"But Monica, won't that be cruel?" Michael countered. "What will happen when he finds out the truth?"

"I will stay with him until the end," Monica said, her voice steady despite the fear swelling in her chest.

Unbeknownst to them, Chandler was standing just outside the door, his feet barely making a sound on the polished floor. He'd heard everything.

A moment later, Monica stepped out of Michael's room, and the sight of Chandler standing there froze her in place. The surprise in her eyes was unmistakable.

"Chandler..." she whispered.

His heart sank, but he said nothing. Without a word, he turned and started walking, and Monica quickly fell in step beside him. Together, they made their way outside to the car, the silence between them thick and fragile.

Once inside, the soft click of the doors closing felt deafening. Monica risked a glance at him, her stomach twisting with nerves.

"Did you... did you hear anything?" she asked hesitantly, her voice small in the quiet car.

Chandler's jaw tensed. His fingers clenched around the steering wheel before he turned to face her, the hurt in his eyes unmistakable. "Yes," he said, his voice rough with emotion. "I heard everything. How could you lie about something like this?"

Monica's throat tightened. "Chandler... please," she whispered, reaching for his hand. "Just calm down and listen to me."

He didn't pull away, though the tension in his grip was unmistakable.

"I didn't mean to hurt you," Monica continued, her voice trembling.

"I just... I wanted you to have hope. The doctor said there's still a good chance after the chemotherapy, and maybe a surgery later. I didn't want to scare you. I was afraid if you knew how serious it was, you'd push me away again. I wanted us to have this — to get married, to be happy."

Chandler's expression softened, though the storm in his chest still raged.

Monica took a steadying breath and added, "If you want... we can move the wedding date forward, while they run more tests, whatever you need."

For a long moment, Chandler didn't speak. He looked out through the windshield at the gray, overcast sky. Then, slowly, he reached over and took her hand in his.

"No," he said quietly, his grip firm. "I want to go ahead. I'm not giving up, Monica. I'll take part in every trial, travel anywhere on Earth if it means finding a cure. I'll fight this to the very end. And no matter what happens, I won't let go of your hand."

His voice cracked on the last words, and Monica's eyes filled with tears. "I promise you that," Chandler whispered.

Monica leaned over and wrapped her arms around him, burying her face in his shoulder. And in that fragile, uncertain moment — beneath the weight of fear and hope — they held on to each other like they were the only solid thing left in the world.

***

Chandler and Monica arrived at the wedding reception, the air filled with laughter and chatter. A crowd of guests awaited them, all eager to celebrate this special moment.

Anna made her way toward her boyfriend, her smile wide. She kissed him passionately, and for a moment, the world seemed to pause around them. Irena stood nearby, her eyes scanning the room until she saw her son with her husband. The boy came running toward her, his face alight with joy. She bent down to pick him up, her heart swelling as he kissed her cheek.

Sophia entered the mansion, her eyes immediately falling on Monica. There she stood in her beautiful wedding dress, looking nervous but stunning.

"You look so beautiful," Sophia said her voice full of warmth and admiration.

Monica smiled, her nerves momentarily calming as she met Sophia's gaze.

Irena approached Chandler, her voice light but serious. "What are your wedding vows?"

Chandler took a deep breath, standing tall. "Yes."

The crowd erupted in laughter as Chandler continued, his voice filled with sincerity.

"This woman…" he began, his eyes never leaving Monica, "knows how to treat others sincerely. She's also…good at caring, comforting them. She is my precious, lovely wife. I love you, Monica."

Monica's heart swelled and she smiled softly before responding, her voice steady but full of emotion.

"Love turns you into the other person. As I dated you, I came to like the things you liked. The time I spent with you, our tastes, feelings—everything became me. At first, it was all yours, but now, it's mine. They say before falling in love, a man isn't a man, and a woman isn't a woman. Through knowing you, I've become a woman... Thank you."

The crowd cheered, urging them to kiss. Chandler, his eyes filled with love, leaned in and kissed Monica deeply.

After the ceremony, Chandler and Monica arrived at their apartment, the echoes of the wedding celebrations still fresh in their minds.

They stood at the door for a moment, both overwhelmed by the day's events. Chandler pulled Monica into a warm embrace, their lips meeting in a kiss that spoke of everything unsaid.

In the soft glow of the room, Chandler lifted Monica into his arms and carried her to the kitchen table. As they began to undress each other, Chandler knelt to remove Monica's boots. When one finally came loose, he fell back onto the floor, letting out a victorious laugh. He quickly returned to kissing her, the energy between them palpable.

The following day, Monica's friends—Irena, Sophia, and Anna—threw her a baby shower. The room was filled with laughter, decorations, and baby presents. Monica stood there, touched by their thoughtfulness.

"Thank you," Monica whispered, her voice full of emotion.

Chandler stood nearby, smiling as he watched them.

"Please don't treat me like a patient in the future," he joked. "Just act like you did today."

Irena smiled softly, her eyes full of understanding. "We're all going to pray for a miracle."

"I'm not praying for a miracle," Chandler replied firmly, "I'm Chandler. I'll make one myself."

***

Later, Chandler and Monica spent some quiet time at the beach, walking hand in hand along the shoreline. The sun was warm, and the sound of the waves was calming.

"Please sing a song for me," Chandler requested, his voice gentle.

Monica hesitated, shaking her head. "I can't sing, and I don't know any songs anyway."

But despite her shyness, she began to sing, her voice sweet and soft, capturing Chandler's heart. A few moments later, they sat together in silence, hands clasped, a smile slowly spreading across Monica's face. Chandler leaned over and kissed her forehead gently.

Monica couldn't help but wonder what would happen if Chandler didn't survive the illness. *No, I can't think like that*, she scolded herself silently. *He'll be fine. He'll be fine. He promised he'd make it through this. He promised.*

But Chandler's voice interrupted her thoughts, his words both vulnerable and strong. "What happens if I can't beat the illness?" he asked quietly.

Then, shaking his head, he continued, "No. Wait and see. I'll work a miracle. I'll save myself. Now that I've met you, and I have you... it's too unfair if I die. It's too unfair, so I can't die."

Monica's heart ached, but she held onto his words, trying to believe them as much as he did. The fear still gnawed at her, but she wouldn't let it take hold.

Suddenly, Chandler's breathing became labored, and he started to lose strength. Monica's stomach dropped. No, she thought desperately. This can't be happening. They rushed him to the hospital.

Doctors and nurses hurried down the hallway, pushing Chandler into the ICU. Monica stood at the entrance, her tears flowing freely as she watched them disappear behind the doors.

Monica sat in the waiting area, her hands clasped tightly in her lap. She could feel the weight of the uncertainty pressing down on her, but she stayed still, hoping that Michael's words were true.

When Michael finally emerged from the ICU, his face was calm but his eyes betrayed a hint of concern. He gave her a reassuring smile.

"It's okay," Michael said, his voice steady. "He'll get better soon. Everything will be better soon."

Monica nodded, but her anxiety remained.

Monica lay beside Chandler's hospital bed, her body pressed close to his. She had not left his side for hours, her exhaustion forgotten in the quiet moments she spent holding him.

Chandler underwent tests in the MRI machine, the whirring sound of the machine filling the room. Monica stood on the other side of the glass, watching, her heart heavy with worry.

Lord, thank you for letting me meet Chandler. I'll do my best for him. And really, truly, thank you for our baby. When I think of how much he suffered alone, my heart aches. Please, Lord, help me. Take care of Chandler. Make him healthy so that later, I'll come to church holding their hands—the three of us.

Michael, Rachel, Monica, and the cancer specialist gathered in a small consultation room. They spoke in hushed tones, their faces grim, but hope still lingered in the air.

A nurse inserted a needle into Chandler's arm, preparing him for a mastectomy to remove the tumor. The sterile lights of the operating room were harsh, but Monica's thoughts were elsewhere—on Chandler, on their future.

Chandler lay in Monica's arms, his body weary but his spirit unbroken. Monica held him close, whispering words of comfort and love, willing him to get better.

Monica lay in bed, Chandler holding their newborn baby in his arms. The joy in the room was palpable, a new life beginning, a family finally whole.

.

Chandler and Monica sat in a quiet park, watching their toddlers—a boy and a girl—run toward them. Chandler scooped them both up, lifting them high into the air. He kissed Monica on the cheek, a soft smile on his face.

It's beautiful, but dreamlike, Chandler thought, as he looked at his family, realizing just how much he had been given.

Back in the hospital, Chandler lay in Monica's arms, his eyes tearful as he woke up.

This must be a dream, right? he thought, his mind foggy. But it's a happy dream, so I'll sleep a little longer…

He gazed at Monica, his heart full of love. Thank you, Monica, for being by my side from that day until this very moment.

With a final sigh, Chandler closed his eyes, letting sleep take over.

Manufactured by Amazon.ca
Acheson, AB